One Shot Too Many

Venkat Raman V

Ukiyoto Publishing

All global publishing rights are held by

Ukiyoto Publishing

Published in 2024

Content Copyright © Venkat Raman V

ISBN 9789367951446

*All rights reserved.
No part of this publication may be reproduced,
transmitted, or stored in a retrieval system, in any form
by any means, electronic, mechanical, photocopying,
recording or otherwise, without the prior permission of
the publisher.*

The moral rights of the authors have been asserted.

*This is a work of fiction. Names, characters, businesses,
places, events, locales, and incidents are either the
products of the author's imagination or used in a fictitious
manner. Any resemblance to actual persons, living or
dead, or actual events is purely coincidental.*

*This book is sold subject to the condition that it shall not by
way of trade or otherwise, be lent, resold, hired out or
otherwise circulated, without the publisher's prior
consent, in any form of binding or cover other than that in
which it is published.*

www.ukiyoto.com

Dedicated to my friends in college who read my early works and acted as encouraging critics

One Shot Too Many

He lived in the middle of a jungle. This was not a jungle built by trees and filled with animals. It was one that was built of concrete and filled with humans. There were a thousand homes in his building but he did not even know who lived next door. Separated by walls of merely a few inches, people lived isolated lives. Roger lived such a life. Not for the lack of effort but most people were busy with their own lives. His mother had died at his birth, his father died when he was eleven and he had been raised in boarding schools ever since. His father had left behind twenty-one million dollars for him but it was mentioned in his father's will that it would not be his until his son turned twenty-eight. He wondered why his father chose that particular number. He was legally an adult at eighteen but there was nothing they could do. Then again, his father had always been called eccentric as far as his memory served.

He lived in a mortgaged apartment and he had a roommate, Dean. Dean initially paid Roger rent and then just became a live-in guest. Roger did not mind.

He had just enough money while Dean had to support a huge family. Besides, he was a trustworthy person and his only real company. In a world where not many could be trusted, Dean was someone whom he could count on. His name was Roger. He had one vice and only one, Alcohol.

***

Roger looked at his purse and then at the calendar. He had three salary hikes in the last five years. His purse had never been this full at the end of the month. Weekends drained his wallets, proportionate to his salary. This month it was different. He had enough to almost manage the next month's expenses. Priya was the reason for all that. Priya owned a 'hair salon and spa' nearby. He met her a few months ago when she talked him out of choosing a mohawk, telling him honestly that it would not be as cool as he thought it would be. Roger had dated a couple of girls before but Priya was different. She made him comfortable around her. She was a loner like him but she had a spark. He did not know what they shared but he understood that it was something more than any relationship he ever had. He remembered when he told his room-mate about her.

"Dean, I seem to like Priya," he said as they ate dinner watching TV.

"The barber?" asked Dean indifferently, his eyes still stuck on the television. Dean had the ability to be effortlessly sarcastic about almost everything in life. It was not easy for new people to accept that but Roger had grown accustomed to his remarks.

"She's not a barber," he said immediately.

"What is she?" asked Dean.

"She owns a spa. She is a stylist," said Roger.

"She cuts hair?" asked Dean indifferently.

"Yeah," said Roger slowly.

"She's a barber. You like her?" asked Dean, still watching television.

"I do," he said.

"Okay," said Dean.

"Okay?" asked Roger in disbelief.

"What do you expect me to say?" retorted Dean looking irritated. Roger sought Dean's opinion on most of his decisions and Dean hated that.

"What do you think?" asked Roger pointedly.

"She got you to reduce drinking. That is not easy. I think she is good for you," he said and got engrossed in the program on the television. Roger grinned widely.

"Sooner or later, you are going to have to introduce me to her," he added quietly.

***

Seven months passed and Roger got serious with Priya. Priya was the best girlfriend he could have hoped for. Priya was a tom-boy so she found no qualms with most of the things about him. Roger could look at other women even when she was with him, play video games with her, watch sports as long as he wanted and best of all, they could hang out without having to talk. They even supported the same team which brought them even closer. Priya was the opposite of needy but there were two things that she could not accept, drinking and smoking. Her father had been an alcoholic and she knew enough to fear it.

"Not even a little?" asked Roger with his eyes wide open.

"If we are getting serious, then no. I understand that you must do what you want to do but I cannot live with someone who drinks or smokes," said Priya calmly.

Roger did not like cigarettes himself but he loved booze. A large part of his life involved getting drunk on weekends and hitting the gym on weekdays to lose the beer belly. It was not one of those clichéd cases where she made him want to stop. It was her or the booze. Roger liked her too much to choose booze. He tried negotiating for once a month but to no avail.

"Trust me. I know. It never stops with one drink," said Priya calmly.

"I am not going to be like your father," said Roger curtly.

"You will if you don't stop. There are people who can control their alcohol. You are not one of them. It pains me to say this but you need to make a choice if we are taking things forward. Me or booze?" asked Priya nervously. She knew that she was making a huge demand but she also knew Roger well by now. Addiction was in his genes.

"Okay. I'll stop drinking," said Roger a few weeks after being given the choice. He had thought a lot about it. He did not want to make a promise that he would not keep. He was going to stop drinking forever.

"You will?" asked Priya with raised eyebrows. She could not believe it but she saw that he was serious.

"I'll drink one last time. I am not talking about my usual weekends. I mean really get drunk. Once and then I'll stop for you," he said.

"Just once? You mean that?" she asked.

"I am doing this for you so you must come with me this weekend. Let me drink one last time and you can bring me home," he said putting his arm around her shoulders.

"Last time you got drunk in my presence, you tried acting smart with me in public," she said, pushing him away.

"Oh, come on. That was a one-time thing. Besides, if I try to sleep with someone wouldn't you feel better if it was you?" he asked.

"I can't think of a reason to refuse," she said, ruffling his hair.

"So, you'll come?" he asked hopefully.

"Sure. You are giving up something huge for me. I can do this," she said.

"This is going to be my last time so I will get absolutely hammered, mind you. I might be setting a few records," he said but she did not mind. This was much better than the alternative.

***

Roger drank that night choosing an assortment of drinks. The assortment included the most expensive drink on the menu and he had everything he wanted including a 'shot challenge' where he set a new personal best. After puking thrice, he had enough. Loading himself with breath mints after, he followed Priya out of the bar. Just as she got to the car, he caught her hand.

"Just one kiss," he said, pulling her closer.

"No. You just puked. I'm not kissing you now. Wait till we get ...," she began.

"I took a handful of breath mints. Come on! Just give me one. You can kiss my cheek if you want," he said, trying to convince her.

She hesitated for a moment and then came forward to kiss his cheek only for Roger to turn to face her at the last moment to make their lips meet. They giggled but did not break the kiss. Roger had kissed women before but nothing ever felt like this. He extended his arms and took a few steps back, feeling like the king of the world. He closed his eyes and swayed happily when he heard rushing footsteps.

"Really?" began Priya when he heard her voice stop abruptly.

As he turned, he saw it. Dazed as he was, he could see three masked men grab Priya. One of them placed a cloth on her face and she stopped struggling. It took him a moment to realize what was going on. He shouted and ran after them. They got into a car and raced away. Roger noted the number and ran towards his car.

The police station was all that he could think of. He ran in reeking in the smell of puke and alcohol. A cop looked at him in disgust and asked, "Lost your way home?"

"My girlfriend was kidnapped," he shouted.

"Calm down. When?" asked the cop getting up from his seat. Just as they spoke, the sergeant came near hearing raised voices.

"A few minutes ago. Outside 'Nighthaven Pub'. There were three men with masks who grabbed her. They went in a white sedan 4BEX972. I don't remember the model. Her name is Priya. She's my girlfriend," he said breathlessly.

The sergeant looked at him seriously. He was half crying. "Get a statement from him. Also, check how drunk he is," he said walking out.

Roger blew into the meter. He was halfway through the statement when the sergeant returned looking suspicious.

"What was the number on the license plate?" asked the sergeant with raised eyebrows.

"4BEX972," said Roger immediately.

"How drunk is he?" asked the sergeant in an undertone to the other cop.

"Very drunk," he replied.

"Give me your car keys," said the sergeant.

Roger handed them over. He went out and there was the sound of a car alarm. The sound continued for a few moments and then stopped. The sergeant returned looking furious. Without any warning, he slapped Roger hard on the face.

"Drunken scoundrel! Do you take us for fools?" he shouted angrily and flung the keys on the table. "The number he says is his own car"

"I swear to you. I was out with my girlfriend. Her name is Priya. She was kidnapped," said Roger desperately.

"Do you have her number?" asked the sergeant.

"Here," he said, handing over his phone.

The sergeant went out of earshot and spoke for about a minute. He returned and said, "There is nobody by name Priya on the other end. Some woman answered".

"Impossible," said Roger desperately.

"You are in no condition for me to believe you. You are lucky I am not arresting you either. Stay here and if you remember something in the morning, we can proceed', he said.

"Impossible," began Roger angrily.

"That wasn't a request," he said menacingly. "I cannot let you drive back in this condition. Stay here and if you remember something in the morning, we can investigate further"

"No, I'm telling you …," began Roger angrily.

"Do not make the mistake of thinking that I am asking you. You will rest now. The interrogation room or in the cell is your choice," he said hotly.

Roger glared angrily at the sergeant but he was helpless. He cursed everyone at the station under his breath and lay down on the dusty bench in the dimly lit room. He lay there staring blankly at the ceiling. After several hours, he dozed off.

***

"Wake up," shouted a cop roughly jerking him awake. He was lying under the bench.

"Here are your keys. Next time we will charge you. If you want to get hammered, take a cab like everyone else," said the sergeant.

"Sir. My girlfriend was kidnapped," said Roger.

"Are you still drunk?" asked the sergeant angrily.

"I swear I am not. I know that she is missing," he said.

After a few minutes of Roger pleading, he was driving the sergeant towards the pub he had been in the night before. The sergeant did not look too happy to ride along but he did not want to take any chances with the case.

"Where was she taken?" asked the sergeant as Roger parked the car.

"Here," he said pointing to the spot where she was taken. After looking around for a few minutes, the sergeant took Roger inside to question the staff.

"Do you have any CCTV cameras here?" asked the sergeant.

The attender showed them to a room on the rear side. The very first clip showed Roger sitting on one corner of the screen, drinking heavily. He seemed to be talking to someone but they were not within the frame.

"Where's the feed for the other side of this image?" asked the sergeant.

"There is no feed for that," said the attender.

"Why not?" asked the sergeant.

"We run a bar. One camera is enough. All we want to check is the register," he said and pointed to the feed.

"Did you see this guy yesterday?" asked the sergeant.

"I see many people come and go. This is a busy place. I can't remember them all. I see him on the screen here. I remember seeing him a few times before but I cannot be sure about yesterday," he said.

"Who will know?" asked the sergeant.

"The bartender might. The others will only know what I know," he said.

They headed to a room where the bartender was sleeping. He woke up looking irritated and angry but refrained from cursing when he saw the sergeant. When he had freshened up, the sergeant asked him, "Do you know him?"

"I see him here often but I don't know him," he replied politely.

"Was he with a woman yesterday?" asked the sergeant.

"He kept coming for drinks repeatedly but I do not know if there was a woman with him," said the bartender.

"She doesn't drink so I kept coming alone," said Roger.

"How much did he drink?" asked the sergeant, ignoring Roger.

"A lot. Maybe I can check," said the bartender.

"Are you sure you were not hallucinating?" asked the sergeant suspiciously.

"I will take you to her workplace now," said Roger. In fifteen minutes, they were outside Priya's spa. As they went in, business was running as usual.

"Where is Priya?" asked Roger to one of the staff.

"I am Priya. How can I help you?" said a middle-aged woman from behind them.

"You … You're not Priya," said Roger in surprise.

"Stop joking around now. I've been styling you for a few months now. What's the matter Roger?" she asked looking puzzled.

"No. Priya … My girlfriend runs this place," said Roger.

"Did you have too much to drink as usual?" she asked as if she knew him very well. She placed an arm on his shoulder which made Roger flinch.

"You know him? You know about his drinking?" asked the sergeant.

"I wouldn't call it a problem. He works in one of those software companies and parties all weekend. He is a typical party animal," she said.

"No sergeant. She's not the one who is here usually. Something fishy is going on here," said Roger desperately. The woman who called herself Priya was looking at them with a confused expression but she did not say anything.

"Who else that you know has seen her? Does anyone know about her? Prove to me that she exists," said the sergeant as he took him away.

With his only hope being his roommate, he phoned Dean. Being questioned, he spoke. His voice echoed on the speakerphone saying, "Priya is his girlfriend. He says they have been going out for a while," said Dean.

"What do you mean he says? Have you met her?" asked the sergeant.

"No, I have not but she is all that he talks about," said Dean.

"His blood alcohol level last night was 0.24. is it possible that he imagined things?" asked the sergeant.

As Roger stared in disbelief, Dean asked, "Imagined what?"

"He says that she was kidnapped," said the sergeant.

"Roger will not lie about something like that even if he was drunk. He drinks like a fish but he can hold his alcohol," said Dean.

"Do you know anything about her?" asked the sergeant.

"She's a stylist. He visits her spa. She has no family. She lives in her spa I believe or spends most of her time there. I don't know much about this," he said.

"I'll call you if I need anything," said the sergeant and turned to Roger. "This guy lives with you but he hasn't even seen your girlfriend? I don't understand your generation. Do you know someone else who can vouch for you?" he asked seriously.

"Vouch?" asked Roger in surprise.

"I doubt if you are mentally stable. I need to leave you with …," began the sergeant.

"My friend just told you …," began Roger hotly.

"Your friend told me that he has never actually seen this woman. The only claim that he makes is that you speak about her. I doubt your mental stability. Now tell me. Can anyone else vouch for you?" asked the sergeant in a stern voice.

Roger meekly replied saying the only name that came to his mind. "Justin, my family lawyer"

"I will leave you at his place," said the sergeant. Roger nodded and drove towards his lawyer's house. He did not know how he was going to explain this to him. He was also getting nervous. Priya had been taken hours ago and nobody was doing anything.

Justin Barnes was a semi-famous lawyer who was also Roger's guardian. He was presently the caretaker of his inheritance. When they reached his house, Justin was reading the newspaper. He looked in surprise as Roger walked in with a cop. Roger stood aside as the sergeant told the lawyer what happened.

"He's a typical bachelor with a good job and enough money. He drinks but he does pretty well at work. I don't think he drinks to a dangerous level," said Justin.

Roger keenly listened to the conversation as Justin's daughter Sophie brought him coffee.

"He had a blood alcohol level of 0.24 last night," said the sergeant.

"Why are cops here?" asked Sophie, coming closer.

"Nothing serious," said Roger trying to shush her so that he could eavesdrop on the conversation. It did not help.

"Big party huh?" she asked as she punched him playfully.

Roger sipped the coffee which helped him feel a little better but he knew that Priya was really missing. The coffee just made that clearer to him. Sophie got the cup from him and waited to chat. On seeing that he was still trying to eavesdrop on the conversation, she left.

In a few minutes, the sergeant returned with Justin. "Take care. I better not find you drunk again," said the sergeant sternly.

"I promise but we still have not found Priya," said Roger.

"Get him checked Mr. Justin," said the sergeant indifferently and left. Roger stood with disbelief. The sergeant seemed perfectly convinced that Roger was insane. Roger attempted to follow him but Justin placed his hand on his shoulder to stop him.

"Where are you going?" asked Justin as Roger tried to leave.

"Out," said Roger not wanting to say that he was going out in search of Priya.

"Take Sophie with you," said Justin.

"Why?" asked Roger angrily. "Don't you trust me?"

"I trust you but I have to be careful too. You know I care for you. Please take her with you. She's on leave today and she will only keep bothering me if she is here. She can keep you company wherever you go," said Justin.

Reluctantly, Roger agreed. Sophie was just out of college. She was extremely childish and too flirty for her own good. Roger had known her for most of his life. They were close but he considered her to be annoying. He kept her company at times out of respect for Justin. She sat jabbing at the stereo as he drove towards the pub where Priya was kidnapped.

"Where are we going?" she asked after about an hour and half.

"I don't know," he said honestly.

"What happened? Why did the cop come with you?" asked Sophie.

"I went to a party last night. My girlfriend was kidnapped there. I went to the cops but they did not believe me. They think that I am crazy. I assure you. I am not. My girlfriend was kidnapped and I need to find her," said Roger.

"Wow. You really have a girlfriend! Miracles do happen," she remarked but stopped as she saw his face. "Why don't they believe you?" she asked slowly.

Roger pulled over and began to recount what happened the night before. His memory was hazy but he was sure that Priya was kidnapped.

"You really have a girlfriend. Are you sure?" she asked.

"Yes. I know I do," said Roger.

"Why would Dean lie?" she asked.

"Dean did not lie," said Roger.

"You are in love with a girl and your roommate has not seen her?" she asked sharply.

"Nobody has," he said.

"How can nobody ….," began Sophie.

"She runs her spa alone. I meet her there. When we ate together, we ordered in. We haven't gone out much. Well … We went out now and then but nowhere relevant," he said.

"What about pictures?" she asked.

"What about them?" he asked.

"Don't you have any with her?" she asked.

"I changed my phone last week. We do not have more than a couple of pictures," he said.

"WhatsApp or SMS chats with her?" she asked.

"Yes," said Roger, taking his phone out hurriedly. He opened the App but the conversation was blank. "No," he groaned.

"Did you clear it?" she asked.

"I don't know," said Roger doubtfully. "I might have"

"Your breath still stinks. How much did you drink last night?" she asked, moving a little away with a look of mild disgust.

"Too much," he said.

"You puked too, didn't you?" she said, shaking her head.

After her insistence, they went to his apartment and he freshened up. "There was a boy who ran errands for her. I don't remember his name but he worked many jobs in the area," he said after some thought.

"Are you sure?" asked Sophie doubtfully as she switched on the TV.

"I hope so," he said, hoping that he was right. He was not sure what was happening. He knew that Priya was real. The feelings that he had for her could not be mistaken.

An hour passed in silence. Neither of them wanted to talk. Roger kept thinking hard about anything that he may have missed. Priya did not have a digital presence and there was no profile picture for her WhatsApp account. The woman at the spa looked nothing like Priya.

"Is there a possibility that you may be imagining her?" asked Sophie.

"No," came a voice from the entrance. Dean stood looking breathless with his bag at the door. He looked grave.

"You returned early," said Roger.

"A cop called me. I thought you were in trouble. I left immediately," he said as he took a seat. "You really should keep the door closed," he said as he shut the door. "There is no way Priya is his imagination. He has cut down on his drinking due to her. I am here every day. If something was wrong with him, I'd know," said Dean.

"They say that mental problems are known last to the people closest to the patient," said Sophie slowly.

"Mental problems? Are you saying that I am mad?" asked Roger bewildered.

"We are just considering possibilities," said Sophie.

"You are considering possibilities. I know him. He is fine," said Dean dismissively.

"Perhaps we should find that boy who helps out at her store," said Sophie.

Roger sat in the backseat as they drove to Priya's store. He did not know what was happening and he was scared. Priya was kidnapped and there was no trace of her. Dean coming back gave him a bit of hope.

"I thought I'd find you here," came a familiar voice. The sergeant came towards them as Roger got out of the car. "Take some rest boy," he told Roger and turned to Dean. "Who are you?" he asked.

"We spoke on the phone. I'm his roommate," said Dean.

"Why are you here?" asked the sergeant.

"He wanted to check something," said Dean.

"Make sure that he doesn't cause any trouble," said the sergeant. He looked suspiciously for a moment and then walked away.

All the other shops in the building were closed. Priya's spa was open but he did not know where the real Priya was. Dean went inside to enquire and came back looking surprised. He returned looking solemn.

"Is there a possibility that this is the real Priya?" asked Dean.

Roger and Sophie looked at him with surprise.

"She says you come here too often and that you are obsessed with her. She asked the sergeant for protection which explains why he is here," said Dean.

"What makes you doubt me?" asked Roger.

"She showed me your WhatsApp chat history. She says she was friends with you but blocked you as you became too flirty. She says that you are harmless but her actions say that she is afraid of you," he said.

"Wait. When the sergeant tried calling her last night, someone answered and said there was nobody called Priya. How does she have my chats now?" asked Roger sharply.

"Someone called her late at night using your phone. She was obviously scared," said Dean.

"She told you that?" asked Roger.

"I assumed that," said Dean.

"Don't assume things," snapped Roger angrily.

"What am I supposed to do? You ... I don't know what to think anymore. I was so sure that you had found someone. Now, I don't know," said Dean.

"Priya is real, Dean. Something fishy is going on," said Roger seriously.

"This isn't a conspiracy," said Dean when Justin's car arrived.

Looking at the people staring at each other, Justin said softly, "Roger, why don't you come with me?" asked Justin softly.

"Where are we going?" asked Roger.

"There's a friend of mine, a doctor. Let's pay him a visit," said Justin as though he was talking to a child.

"Really? A doctor? Do you really think I'm insane? I don't need a psychiatrist," he said hotly. All three looked at him anxiously. "Fine," he said angrily. "I'll go". He was irritated that even people in his close circles were thinking that he was mad. They were wasting time worrying about his sanity when they were supposed to be looking for Priya.

Roger sat silently as they drove to the doctor's place. He was angry at all three of them though it was nobody's fault. He could not understand what was happening.

He had to speak to the psychiatrist who bored him with pointless questions. He came out grumpy and anxious realizing that Priya was still gone and he was wasting time. He tried to go from there but he was subdued and given an injection.

Roger woke to find himself in his room. It took a while for everything to come into focus. He felt tired from the meds and stared blankly at the ceiling.

"Hey," said Dean who looked like he had been sitting beside him for a long time.

"Hey," said Roger weakly.

"The doctor reckons this is only temporary insanity. You are perfectly sane now but all that may have been caused due to too much booze. He says you should be fine after a couple of days of rest," said Dean.

"Priya?" asked Roger hopefully.

"Nothing on that. Maybe you are obsessed with that old woman. Maybe things went into an overdrive," said Dean.

"Did you assume that?" asked Roger sarcastically.

"Don't be like that. Maybe this is for the better," said Dean reasonably.

"I drink once or twice a week. I lead a healthy lifestyle otherwise. I don't smoke or do drugs. I've been telling you about Priya for a few months now. Do you really think I am mad?" asked Roger.

"I don't know what to think anymore," said Dean.

"What if I really am mad?" said Roger slowly.

"You are not mad. This is just a one-time thing," said Dean immediately. "Slow down on the booze and it will be fine"

"Last night was supposed to be my last time drinking," said Roger sadly.

"It will all become good. Take some rest," said Dean patting Roger's shoulder.

***

Dean and Roger woke up to the sound of the doorbell ringing. It was close to 2 : 00 AM. Sleepily, Dean opened the door to find the sergeant standing outside.

"Sergeant?" he said in surprise.

"Where's your friend?" asked the sergeant hurriedly.

"Tell me," said Roger getting up.

"I believe you," said the sergeant staring at Roger's face.

"Believe what?" asked Roger doubtfully.

"Your girlfriend is real. She may be kidnapped," he said, closing the door behind him. He helped himself to water from the fridge and took a seat.

"Why do you believe me now?" asked Roger.

"I saw a little boy flee when he saw you. He looked guilty. When I caught him, he said something fishy was going on. When I called up that night, a voice said there was nobody called Priya. The woman pretending to be the owner asked me for protection but she is nowhere to be seen now. I don't know where I have seen that woman but I remember seeing that face somewhere. Not in a good way. Also ... Is this the real Priya?" asked the sergeant showing a small photo.

"Yes. How ...?" began Roger happily.

"The phone company had her records. I went to her place. It was locked. The shopkeepers nearby know nothing. Something is really fishy here," he said.

"Sorry," said Dean, turning to Roger.

"No time for that. Please help me find her," said Roger to the sergeant.

"I still have the complaint you wrote. My men are on it as we speak. As of now, I am treating it as a missing person case. I need you to help me with a few details," he said.

"Sure," said Roger briskly.

"Does she have any enemies?" he asked.

"No. Nobody even knows her except her customers. That could explain why the other shopkeepers do not know her. She works alone and there is this boy who does odd jobs for her. I see that you have met him," said Roger. They had made little progress but he felt as though they had rescued Priya already. For the first time since she was kidnapped, someone was believing him.

"Did she have any problems with anyone? Her spa is in a prime location which is often a good motive. Any information would be helpful," said the sergeant.

"No. She rents the place from a woman. They are on good terms. There is nobody who would want to hurt her," he said confidently.

"There has to be something. Kidnaps are never random. People don't know she's going out with you. Even if they did, you are not married," said the sergeant.

"What's that supposed to mean?" asked Roger hotly.

"It means she is nobody. There is no possibility of a ransom. What about you? Are you from money?" asked the sergeant, staring at him.

"Yes but I will not be getting it for a year," said Roger and explained how he would not get his inheritance until he turned twenty-eight.

"Who all know that you will be getting this money?" asked the sergeant.

"Nobody. Most people have no idea who I am. My school and college records have Justin as my guardian. Only he and Dean know about this," said Roger.

"You trust him?" asked the sergeant pointing at Dean.

"Hey," began Dean, looking annoyed.

"He is like a brother to me," said Roger dismissively.

"Let me start enquiring around. Keep your phone on at all times. I will call you if I need information," said the sergeant. He walked to the door, hesitated and said, "Don't get drunk again. I need you conscious"

"Don't worry. I am never drinking again for the rest of my life," said Roger emphatically.

The sergeant looked indifferent but nodded slowly before he left.

***

"The sergeant now believes him. He is searching for her," said Dean. He and Roger sat at Justin's garden early the next morning.

"This is wonderful. I'm glad you are not insane," said Justin looking relieved.

Roger stared blankly at the garden. It was more than forty-eight hours since Priya had been taken. He had no clue who had taken her or where she was now. He tried hard not to think what they could have done to her.

"What do you know about her?" asked Justin.

"Huh …," asked Roger as he came out of his daze.

"What of her family?" asked Justin.

"She does not mention her father. I don't think he's alive. Her mother died two years ago. She leased the place with the insurance money," said Roger.

"Siblings?" asked Justin sharply.

"Nobody," said Roger.

"Does she know that you are going to get a huge inheritance?" asked Justin.

"Yes but do not say what you are thinking. She is not running a con on me. Besides, the money is untouchable now," said Roger.

"Not exactly," said Justin immediately.

"What do you mean?" asked Roger.

"According to the will, I can withdraw any amount that you want. As I am the caretaker, I can access it," he said.

"You lawyers and your loopholes. Let me figure out how to find her and then we can figure out the amounts that you will withdraw for me," said Roger walking towards his car.

"Don't do anything stupid," called Justin as they drove off.

"Why do people suspect my loved ones? The sergeant doubted you and Justin doubts Priya. What's wrong with these people?" hissed Roger.

"It's a natural response," said Dean soothingly.

"It is bullshit," he snapped. "Will they suspect me next?"

"When there is money involved, nobody can be trusted. It is the way of the world. The job of a cop is to doubt," said Dean.

"Money. Hmpf," scoffed Roger shaking his head. "Would you screw me over for my inheritance?" he asked.

"I'm not going to answer that question," said Dean.

"Exactly. Instead of looking at culprits they keep looking at us," he said.

Just as he said that, his phone rang. It was the sergeant. "Can you come to the station immediately?" he asked.

In five minutes, they had reached the station. "I have checked the status of every known kidnapper here. Everyone has been checked. Nobody has kidnapped your girl," said the sergeant.

"What does that mean?" asked Roger.

"It means either she was kidnapped by someone outside the usual list of suspects or ...," he said and paused with his eyebrows raised.

"Or what?" asked Roger.

"Or you blacked out something when you were drunk," said the sergeant.

"No. She was taken. She is still fine," said Roger dismissively. The sergeant asked for a few details but Roger was increasingly distraught.

"Go rest and come back later. You are of no use to this investigation like this," said the sergeant.

As Roger walked to the car, his legs became flaccid. Dean held him to support him but fear took hold of Roger. Priya was gone for long enough now. He now lost all hope. He stared blankly as Dean drove him home.

***

Roger woke up to find Justin at his bedside.

"Where's Dean?" asked Roger.

"I told him to go to work. I offered to stay with you," said Justin.

Roger's phone rang. It was the sergeant.

"Rest. I'll take this one," said Justin while taking the call. He left the room as he answered. He came back looking grave. "It was the sergeant," he said.

"What did he say?" asked Roger.

"He wants you to identify a body," said Justin.

"Why? ... No," groaned Roger, hoping that he had misheard Justin. The inspector had told him that the first seventy-two hours were critical after which they had to be prepared for all possibilities.

"It may not be her. Keep hoping. She may still be alive," said Justin encouragingly.

Roger nodded mechanically but he couldn't face the facts. He felt numb. He could not think of anything clearly.

"Let's go," said Justin, placing his hand gently on Roger's shoulder.

The car moved swiftly and Roger stared outside blankly. After reaching the outskirts, Justin pulled over near a bridge.

"Let's go," he said and pulled over. Roger followed him.

"There," said Justin pointing near the base of the bridge.

"I don't see any police vehicles or sirens. Are we sure that this is the right place?" asked Roger looking around.

"Keep walking. This is the place I was told about," said Justin curtly.

"I don't think we are in the right place. I think we need to call him back," said Roger shaking his head. Roger walked forward when he heard a click. He turned to see Justin holding a gun. He put his hands in the air involuntarily.

Slightly trembling but face contorted in anger, Justin said, "I wish we hadn't come to this"

"What are you doing, Justin?" asked Roger raising his hands in fear.

"You stupid, drunken moron," said Justin stuttering.

"Put the gun down. Let's talk about this," said Roger with panic.

"Talk? You idiot. Do you have any idea how much trouble I went through to …," he shouted furiously.

"Trouble for what?" asked Roger in surprise.

"To prove that you do not have a stable mind," said Justin angrily.

"Why would you do that?" asked Roger. It then struck him. "Yes. That way you would still be the caretaker of my property," he said slowly.

"Caught on, have you?" snapped Justin.

"Why not kill me? Why go through all that effort?" asked Roger.

Justin looked up in surprise. "Do you want to die?" he asked as he steadied the gun.

"I'm just saying ... It would have been easier," said Roger nervously.

"If you die, the money goes to charity. I could siphon it but ... I wanted to avoid killing you," said Justin.

"Why?" asked Roger looking around nervously. There was nothing nearby that he could use to protect himself. He knew that Justin was ready to kill him and he was helpless.

"What do you mean why? You are like a son to me. I wanted to get my daughter married to you but you two never clicked," he said grumpily.

"So, you used my weakness against me?" asked Roger realizing that Justin had planned this well. He used Roger's drinking habit to his benefit and he had done it really well.

"You forced my hand," said Justin.

"Did it occur to you that if you needed money, all you needed to do was ask? I trusted you. You took care of me all these years. I owe you," said Roger earnestly.

"You mean begged you," scoffed Justin. "I deserve that money. I don't need you to give it to me. You'd be nothing if it were not for me. You would have died as a child or grown up to be a nobody. Instead, you were holding a good job and dating a stylist," he said angrily.

"What did you do to her?" asked Roger immediately. This was the first time someone other than him had spoken about Priya since the kidnap.

"Priya's alive but I have to kill you both now," said Justin.

"You are not a killer. You tried so hard not to kill me. Let me and Priya go. Keep my money," said Roger.

"If only it were that simple. Stay still. This will only hurt you if you try to escape," said Justin and aimed with the gun.

"Hands up!" came a loud voice. The sergeant stood on the bridge with his gun aimed at Justin. There were three other cops and Dean was standing behind them looking terrified.

"Don't be stupid. Drop the gun," said the sergeant two cops came closer.

"How?" asked Justin in disbelief.

"The sergeant suspected you. When you sent me away, we had a doubt. When the call to Roger's phone was cut and then the phone was switched off, we confirmed the doubt. We tracked your mobile which was on," said Dean with a smirk. He was enjoying it as he narrated their efforts. He was satisfied that the had saved Roger.

"Where's Priya?" asked Roger as the cop took the gun away.

"In my beach house," said Justin gruffly. He knew that it was over. He was looking to minimize damage now.

"We'll get her," said the sergeant gesturing to his men.

"You were like a father to me," said Roger welling up.

"I should have gone ahead and killed you when it didn't work out with my daughter," spat Justin gravely.

"You'd kill me over a few millions?" asked Roger in disbelief.

"People kill for a lot less," said Justin shaking his head as the cops took him to their car.

"I can't believe you would do this," said Roger tearfully. Justin stared indifferently.

***

Roger sat in his apartment with Dean and a totally devastated Sophie. They had spent the better part of the last two hours consoling her. She could not believe it at first. After she believed it, she could not handle it.

Justin had been arrested. Roger even tried to withdraw his complaint but Dean had stopped him. Justin had kidnapped a person close to Roger and almost killed him. He did not deserve any leniency. Justin had been forced to give them details of the deeds to his inheritance were before going to jail. It was as per the sergeant's instructions. In a few more weeks, he would be rich but that did not matter to him now. He had been betrayed by someone he respected as a father.

Just as he sat thinking, the sergeant came to the door. Behind him, he could see the shadow of a woman. As they both came in, he saw her. Covered in dust, a little tired but looking perfectly alright was Priya.

Roger rushed forward with his arms outstretched for a hug.

"Hug your girlfriend, not me," said the sergeant clearly surprised.

"Thank you, Sir. You saved my life and much more," he said.

"Just do me a favour," said the sergeant.

"Anything," said Roger immediately.

"Don't turn up drunk in my station," he said but Roger had already moved on though the others began to laugh.

He held Priya's hand. He gently caressed her face and she closed her eyes. Tears rolled down her eyes as she leaned on Roger's shoulder.

"Dean, this is Priya," he said showing Dean his girlfriend.

"I'm so sorry," he said turning back to Priya but she threw her arms around his neck. "If it weren't for me …," he began.

"I'd still be single," she said completing his sentence.

Dean and Sophie came closer as he introduced Priya properly to them. Everything was back to how it had to be.

* THE END *

About the Author

Venkat Raman V

Venkat Raman V is a banker by profession and a writer by passion. He is an internationally published researcher with a fondness for storytelling. Having written for several magazines and publications, he frequently posts on Instagram on his handle *@VVRamanWrites*. He has an anthology series on Kindle called 'Scribbles in the back-benches'

www.ingramcontent.com/pod-product-compliance
Lightning Source LLC
LaVergne TN
LVHW041640070526
838199LV00052B/3479